My Dress-up Party

by Sarah Willson
illustrated by Jennifer Oxley

Ready-to-Read

Simon Spotlight/Nick Jr.

New York   London   Toronto   Sydney   Singapore

Based on the TV series *Blue's Clues*® created by Traci Paige Johnson,
Todd Kessler, and Angela C. Santomero as seen on Nick Jr.®
On *Blue's Clues,* Joe is played by Donovan Patton. Photos by Joan Marcus.

SIMON SPOTLIGHT
An imprint of Simon & Schuster Children's Publishing Division
1230 Avenue of the Americas, New York, New York 10020
Copyright © 2003 Viacom International Inc. All rights reserved.
NICKELODEON, NICK JR., *Blue's Clues*, and all related titles, logos, and characters are
trademarks of Viacom International Inc.
Manufactured in the United States of America
First Edition
2 4 6 8 10 9 7 5 3 1

Library of Congress Cataloging-in-Publication Data

Willson, Sarah.
My dress-up party / by Sarah Willson.—1st ed.
p. cm.—(Ready-to-read ; #6)
Summary: Blue has a dress-up party but only finds a costume for herself
at the last minute.
ISBN: 0-689-85229-0
[1. Costume — Fiction. 2. Parties — Fiction.]
I. Oxley, Jennifer - ill. II. Title. III. Series.
PZ7.W6845My 2003
[E] 21   2002006030

Hi! I am  BLUE . We are having a dress-up party! Joe is hanging BALLOONS all over the HOUSE .

Mr. Salt and Mrs. Pepper baked a 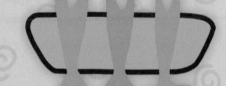.

CAKE

Paprika will scoop out the  . Yum!

ICE CREAM

Now we can set the  **TABLE** with  **PLATES** , **FORKS** ,

and **SPOONS** !

It is time to dress up! Tickety Tock is going as a grandfather  CLOCK.

Mailbox is wearing

a  MAILMAN costume.

Mr. Salt and Mrs. Pepper are dressed up as  CHEFS .

Paprika is going as a .

SPOON

Joe and I still need costumes. We can look in Joe's  .

CLOSET

Maybe his  will give us an idea.

SHOES

He can be a  BASEBALL
player, an ice-skater,
or pretend he is
going to the BEACH .

Look at all the HATS

in my COSTUME BOX .

I could be an  ,

ASTRONAUT

a , or a .

FIREFIGHTER   FARMER

The guests are already at the !

DOOR

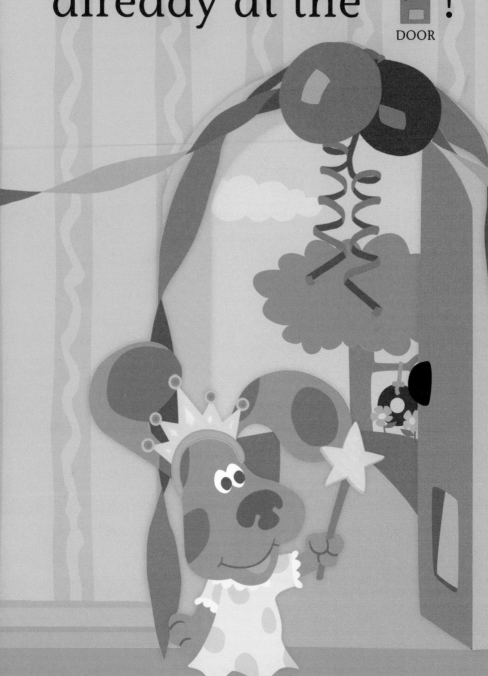

Magenta came as a  PRINCESS .
Periwinkle is wearing a  MAGICIAN costume.

We still need costumes
What else is in
my 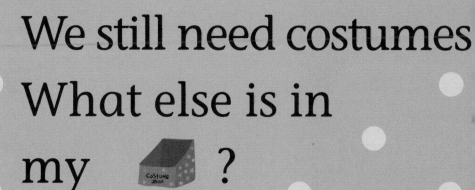 ?

COSTUME BOX

I think Joe has an idea. What could he do with these  ?

SOCKS

Now I am dressed like .

JOE

And Joe is dressed like me, !

BLUE

It is time for  ICE CREAM
and CAKE . Thank you
for coming!

3234503055 38855